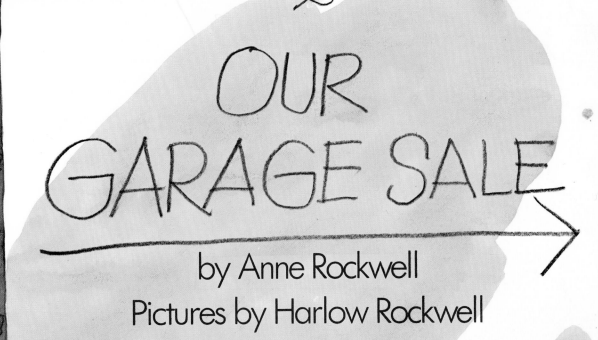

OUR GARAGE SALE

by Anne Rockwell

Pictures by Harlow Rockwell

 Greenwillow Books, New York

Text copyright © 1984 by Anne Rockwell. Illustrations copyright © 1984 by Harlow Rockwell.
All rights reserved. No part of this book may be reproduced or utilized in any form or by any
means, electronic or mechanical, including photocopying, recording or by any information storage
and retrieval system, without permission in writing from the Publisher, Greenwillow Books, a division
of William Morrow & Company, Inc. 105 Madison Avenue, New York, N.Y. 10016.
Printed in the United States of America   First Edition   10 9 8 7 6 5 4 3 2 1

Library of Congress Cataloging in Publication Data
Rockwell, Anne F.   Our garage sale.   Summary: A child describes his family's garage sale.
[1. Garage sales—Fiction. I. Rockwell, Harlow, ill.   II. Title.   PZ7.R59430t 1984   [E]
80-16704   ISBN 0-688-80278-8   ISBN 0-688-84278-X (lib. bdg.)

Our attic was full of
old things.

My father's hockey stick
and skates were there.
He doesn't play hockey
anymore.

My mother's old typewriter
was all dusty in the corner.
She has a new one now.

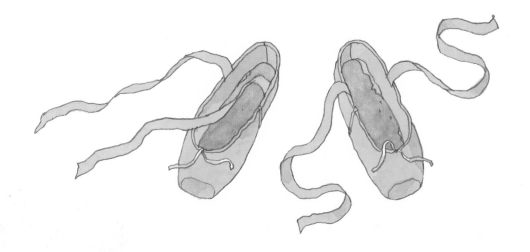

My sister's ballet shoes

were too small for her,

and there were two snowsuits
and a pair of boots
that were too small for me.

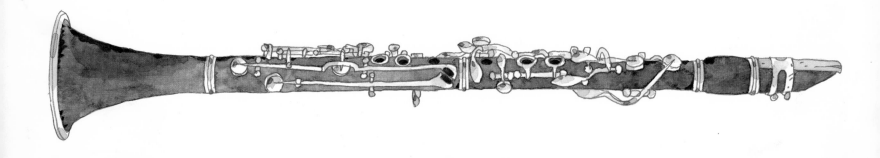

My mother hadn't played
her clarinet
for fifteen years,

and Aunt Martha's chair
was sitting there with a hole
in the seat.

Our attic was full of old things.
They were too good to throw away,
but they were old things.
We didn't have room to keep them
and we didn't need them
anymore.
"Somebody might,"
said my sister.

There were
more old things
in our cellar,

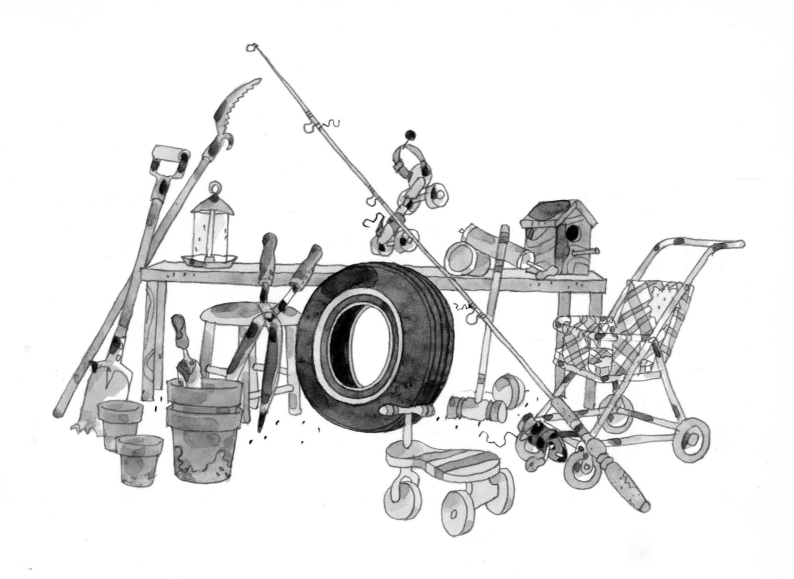

and in our garage too.

So we decided to have
a garage sale
in our driveway.

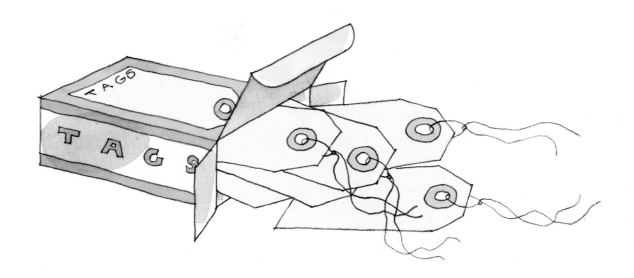

We bought a box of little tags,

and put prices
on everything.

We put signs on
the trees at the corner.

We put them
on the bulletin board
in our supermarket.

It didn't rain on Saturday.

Lots of people came to
our garage sale.

I sold my three puzzles
I had put together too many times,
and I sold my old truck
for ten cents.

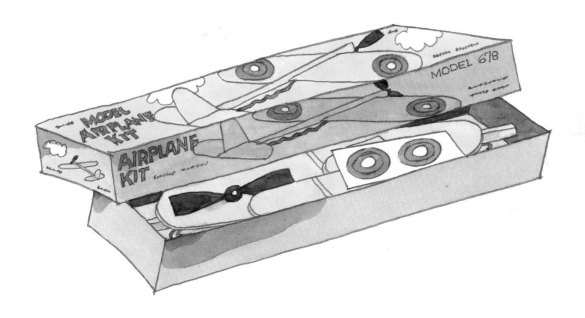

I got enough money
to buy a model airplane kit

and a package of bubble gum too.